CODE NAME MR RIGHT

Takeaways

CODE NAME
MR RIGHT

JACQUELINE HARVEY

Lothian
BOOKS

For the children who inspire me,
for Olivia who listens and
for Ian who believes in me.

Thomas C. Lothian Pty Ltd
132 Albert Road, South Melbourne, 3205
www.lothian.com.au
Author's website: www.jacquelineharvey.com

Copyright © Jacqueline Harvey 2003
First published 2003

National Library of Australia
Cataloguing-in-Publication data:

Harvey, Jacqueline.
Code name Mr Right.

For upper primary school age children.
ISBN 0 7344 0594 4.

I. Title. (Series : Takeaways).

A823.4

Cover design by Michelle Mackintosh
Illustrations by Annie Mertzlin
Text design by Paulene Meyer
Printed in Australia by Griffin Press

CONTENTS

ME

Hi. My name's Penelope and I think that's the dumbest name anyone could ever have. I don't know why my parents chose it. It's disgusting. You can't even shorten it to something better — you just end up with Penny, which is even more stupid. Who names their kid after an old coin? Why couldn't they have called me something like Georgia, or Charlie, or Robbie? I hate soppy girly names and mine's one of the worst ever.

Let me introduce myself properly. As you already know, my first name is Penelope, followed by Estella Grace Scott. Estella after my Gran, and Grace after Nanna. If I thought either of those names was better, I'd use one, but yuck — they're worse! I suppose I'm lucky they're not called Beryl and Flo. My friend Andrew's granny is called Muriel Ethel Edna, so it's just as well he wasn't born a girl. Fancy inheriting one of those names. His mum is pregnant at the moment but we're all hoping that if it's a girl, she won't decide to use any family names. The poor kid will be scarred for life before she even leaves hospital.

I'm just an average kid really. I can say that with confidence because when we studied measurement in maths, everyone in the class had to measure their height and weight. Mr Maslin, my teacher, helped us to work out the averages and well, I was right on for both. I've got sandy blonde hair and greenish–greyish eyes, which my mum says are beautiful but I think are just plain old dull.

I'm ten and a half years old, but I act a lot older than that. I have to. You see, when I was eight my parents split up, so I had to act all grown up and 'get over it', otherwise Mum would have sent me to some stupid doctor who wanted me to talk my head off and cry all over him. I know this because that's what happened to my big brother.

MATT

My brother's name is Matt and he's twelve.
He's a grommet — that's kid-speak for surfie.
He's crazy about surfing, and if he's not
on his board he's glued to the PlayStation.
He's a major pain. I guess you could say he
has problems. Mostly because he's really
upset that Dad left. I think he kind of blames

himself in a way. I've tried to tell him that he has far too high an opinion of his own importance, and that he had nothing to do with Dad leaving, but I don't think he believes me. He needs to chill out and stop taking everything so seriously.

I, of course, know the real reason Mum and Dad split up. It was because they were never really compatible in the first place, they should never have got married, and they only had kids because that was what everyone expected. I know all this because I overheard Mum talking to her sister, Aunty Sandy, one day when I was supposed to be outside playing with my dog.

Well, I *was* outside and then I trod in one of Rolly's disgusting smelly you-know-whats, and I had to sneak inside to wash my runners in the laundry tub. Mum would have killed me — they were brand new. Not only that, the laundry stinks so much sometimes she keeps asking if Matt or I are hiding any stray animals in there. Mum's always suspicious about *really* bad smells in the laundry — I mean, worse than Matt's wet footy socks smell — since the time I caught a mouse and hid him in a shoebox beside the clothes dryer. Unfortunately for Bonzo — that was his name — he must have suffocated from the heat (and well, maybe I didn't put quite enough air holes in the lid because I was afraid he would escape, and then Mum would have a heart attack). It happened when I was on a Joey Scouts sleepover, so I didn't find him for a couple of days. I felt really bad, so I gave him a proper funeral in the backyard and made a little mouse-sized cross and everything. I buried him under the lemon tree because I thought the smell of the lemons might overpower his small but very stinky rotting carcass.

Anyway, I didn't mean to listen in, but when I heard Mum talking about Dad I couldn't help it. It's not like she was being mean or saying anything bad. She even told Aunty Sandy that she still loved him, but more like a brother than a husband. I thought she mustn't have loved him very much, because I can't imagine loving Matt at all. Gross!

I was pretty upset at first when Dad moved out, but now I know it's for the best. There's no fights any more (except for between me and Matt) and I still get to see Dad every second weekend. He has this great girlfriend called Melissa (we call her Mel for short) and Mum says so long as she's kind to Matt and me, that's all that matters. Dad takes us to really cool places and always lets us do what we want. Mum says he's a typical 'Disneyland Dad', but I don't agree. I know he feels bad about them breaking up and he just tries to do his best for us. Besides, he hasn't even talked about taking us to Disneyland yet, but believe me, I'm working on it.

MUM

The most significant adult in my life is, of course, my mum, Francine. Everyone calls her Frankie, and I think she has the coolest name in the world. How someone with a name as great as that ever thought of Penelope for me, I will never understand. I suppose as far as mothers go she's pretty cool too. Apart from her mental attacks over the state of my bed-room, and making me eat lots of disgusting vegetables (which she swears are good for me), she's a great mum. She lets us stay up late on the weekends and she wears trendy clothes. She always tries to make herself look good, and she's really pretty for someone as ancient as thirty-five. I hope I look as young as her when I'm that old.

It was hard for Mum when she and Dad split up. At first she cried a lot, but then she kept telling us not to blame Dad and that it was nobody's fault. Matt didn't believe her and said that Dad was a creep for leaving and that he hated him. Poor Mum — first of all she had to deal with breaking up, and then she had to cope with Matt cracking up.

One day after school, while I was wait-ing for soccer training to start, I overheard a couple of mums talking. Mrs Oliver said, 'Have you seen Francine Scott lately? She is obviously trying to snag a new man.'

It made me so angry. Just because Mum doesn't wear old granny clothes, and she still has beautiful long hair and is really attractive, those two busy-bodies thought she must be trying to find a new husband. I was *so* mad — especially because it just wasn't true. Mum hadn't even been on one date since she and Dad split up.

Mrs Oliver and Mrs George were just a pair of wrinkly old crows with nothing better to do than gossip about other people's lives. So, kind of without thinking about it much, I walked up and asked if they knew where their husbands had been last Friday night. Then I kind of mentioned that I might have seen Mr Oliver talking to a pretty blonde lady at the golf club meat raffle. I know I shouldn't tell stories and, well — it was only a little white lie — I did see him talking to a blonde lady; it just happened that it was Mrs Blair, who's eighty-three and sells the raffle tickets.

Well, you should have seen the look on their faces. It was as if I'd told them their dresses were tucked up into their knickers or they had boogers hanging out their noses. They grabbed their precious little brats from the class below mine and ran away whispering (very loudly), 'Penelope Scott is a rude little madam — who does she think she is?'

I know I shouldn't have been eaves-dropping, but they shouldn't talk about my mum behind her back. Besides, I think they were just really embarrassed that someone caught them saying things they shouldn't have.

Dad

When Mum and Dad split up, Dad moved down the coast to Shelley Beach, about two hours drive away. He said it would be easier on everyone if we weren't all living in the same town — especially when the gossip hotline got going. Believe me, with Mrs Oliver and Mrs George in charge, it didn't take

long before everyone knew what had happened — and what they didn't know they just
made up.

I really miss him, but he phones most
nights and he comes to see us every second
weekend. But it is strange not having him
around. It's the little things that matter the
most — like our Sunday morning routine.
Dad and I used to ride our bikes into town
every Sunday morning, pick up the papers
and buy croissants from the bakery for
breakfast. The first time I went on my own, it
just didn't feel right. I got the papers and
rode straight home. Mr Cameron at the
newsagency must have known that I was a bit
down because he put a mini Freddo in the
middle of the papers and winked at me when
I was leaving. I didn't realise the Freddo was
there until I got home. Mum asked me why
there was a squashed chocolate frog hiding
in the movie guide, and then I understood
what the wink was for.

She didn't even ask where the croissants were. I think she knew that without Dad it just wasn't the same. We started having home-made pancakes instead. It was Mum's way of making things special for the three of us.

When we stay with Dad, we always go out for breakfast and read the papers together. Each of us has our own section — Dad has the serious bits, Matt has sport and I get the cartoons. So after a while, even though Mum and Dad aren't together, life is kind of normal again.

Dad works for an oil company. He's a petrochemical engineer — I don't really understand what that means but I know that he studied science at university and he's really smart. Maybe that's why I like science too. Matt, on the other hand must take after Mum. She's a graphic artist and he loves to draw too. I'm absolutely hopeless at art. When I tried to copy a still-life basket of fruit, Mr Maslin asked what I was doing sketching a rhinoceros. I tried to explain that it was the pineapple, but he just shook his head and grinned.

One night when Dad called, he asked if we'd mind if he brought a friend to meet us on the weekend. I thought it must have been one of his work mates, so I was a bit surprised when this gorgeous red-haired girl got out of the car. He introduced her as Melissa but she said we could call her Mel. I liked her straight away. Matt didn't. He was awful to her. He called her Mel Smell and said that if she thought Dad was really interested in her, she was badly mistaken. He said the minute she got a fat backside Dad would drop her like a hot potato. Matt said that Dad was only trying to make Mum jealous so that they would get back together.

Poor Mel — she never got upset and when Matt was totally foul she always tried to make a joke out of it. But one weekend when Dad took us all to this posh hotel, Matt couldn't help himself and finally pushed Dad too far. First of all he spent the whole day sucking up to Dad and ignoring Mel. He even wrote Dad a note saying that he thought Mel was only using him for his money. He left the note on the bedside table and Mel saw it. She was crying and Dad went off his brain at Matt and told him that he should pull his head in and get used to the fact that she was around.

I'd never seen him so mad. Dad told Matt that he was being a selfish brat and that heaps of kids had parents who got divorced. He said Matt was lucky because Mel liked him even though he was acting like a complete pain in the backside. I was listening in and silently cheering from the bathroom, where I'd been banished. It was about time somebody told Matt to get real and get over it. I guess it started to work. After a few months I think even psycho boy began to realise that she wasn't going away. Dad was really happy and Mel was fantastic. It was kind of like having a big sister — but I didn't tell Mum that.

DOLPHIN SNOrES!

We live at 87 Pacific Vista Drive, Dolphin Shores. I call it Dolphin Snores because nothing exciting ever happens here. We live right near the beach, so I suppose you can always go swimming or check out the rock-pools. It doesn't rain much until around February, and then it pours nearly every afternoon for a month or more. Sometimes we get the tail end of a cyclone, and then the ocean becomes so rough Mum worries that some of the houses along the cliff might fall in. I never worry about that. I think it would be hilarious — some of them need to fall in they're so old and disgusting — and most of the ones closest to the edge are just ancient fishing shacks anyway.

People who've been here forever tell stories about years ago, when the waves were so huge Mr Cameron and his brothers were surfing in the main street, right past their parents' newsagency. Well, it's Mr Cameron's newsagency now, but it always makes me annoyed when I hear stuff like that, because really cool things only ever seemed to happen years ago — even my mum couldn't remember that, and she's lived here all her life too.

So, mostly the sun shines, the folks are cheerful and life is good. Which in my opinion all amounts to a really boring place.

I'd love to live in the city, where people are always going missing and there are sirens and hold-ups and stuff like that.

The best thing that ever happened at Dolphin Shores was last year when a whale beached itself and the Greenies came to try and help move it back into the sea. I loved all the television cameras and reporters. I tried hard to get on TV, but every time I charged in front of the camera the reporter got really narky and told me if I didn't stop it they'd call the police to come and take me home. I didn't care about them calling the police — everyone knows Sergeant Maxwell and he's a top bloke — but I thought Mum would be pretty annoyed if I arrived home in the patrol car. The neighbours — especially Cranky-pants Johnson, would all think the worst, like I'd been caught shoplifting from the newsagency or spraying graffiti on the toilet block at the oval or something just as bad and, well, she'd had enough problems lately.

When you get divorced in a town like Dolphin Shores, everyone wants to make it their business. She didn't need the extra attention.

SCHOOL

I'm in Year 5 and my brother is in Year 6 at Dolphin Shores Primary. Matt repeated Year 3, so that's why we're only one grade apart. I can't wait until next year, because then he goes to high school and I won't have to put up with him any more. There are only two classes in each year, so everyone pretty much knows everyone else. I love school.

My teacher's name is Mr Maslin and he's really cool. I kind of felt sorry for him when he first got transferred to Dolphin Shores. He comes from the city and I told him that he'd probably want to move back there as soon as he could. I warned him that there aren't too many things to do here — unless you like surfing and going to the beach. But he says that he loves it, and it's a great place to bring up kids. I'm glad he likes it, because he's the best teacher I've ever had. He does all these experiments with us, and once when my class was doing a science show in assembly, he made a cork pop out of a bottle and it got stuck in one of the holes in the ceiling. I nearly wet my pants I was laughing so much. Even Mr Nulley thought it was hilarious and allowed Mr Maslin to leave the cork up there as a reminder.

He trains our soccer team too. We were totally pathetic before he came, but now he says at least we don't look like a swarm of bees, all going for the ball at the same time. I scored my first goal a few weeks ago against our arch enemies, the Sandy Bay Stingers. Mum and my friend Kimi were cheering so loudly it was embarrassing — the two of them are always threatening to bring pom-poms and dress up as our cheer squad. I've told them that if they ever do, both of them face a lifetime spectator ban — just like Claire's dad, when he was asked to stay away from our tee-ball games for being a little too enthusiastic.

We have a mixed soccer team, which is fun because I couldn't stand playing with a whole bunch of wussy girls who are worried about breaking a nail. I leave that up to Kimi and she only comes to watch!

My favourite subjects are science, maths and sport. I hate English. It's *sooooo* boring, especially comprehension. We always read these dumb books about fairies and magic. *Pleeeze*, I'd rather clean my bedroom.

That gives you an idea about how much I hate comprehension, because my bedroom looks like it was hit by a cyclone. I just don't see the point in tidying it up all the time — well, any time for that matter. I know where everything is — or at least I usually do.

I hate it when Mum goes on one of her superwoman cleaning missions. Once I tried to keep her out by putting a sign on my door that said, 'Beware, attempting to clean this room may be hazardous to your health!' I thought it was funny, but she went ballistic when she found the mouldy peanut-butter sandwiches under my bed. She said that they had begun to grow into the carpet, and that I *would* contract some kind of deadly disease. I asked her if I could take them to school to use for a science experiment. She gave me her 'evil stare of death' look and I thought I'd better not push my luck. I decided to ask Mr Maslin if I could grow my own mould another time.

KIMI

My best friend's name is Kimi. Yes, that's
right, Kimi. It's not short for Kimberly or
long for Kim. It's just Kimi. We've been
friends since Year 2, although we did have a
rocky start to our relationship.

It was the first day of school and Kimi
had just moved to Dolphin Shores (poor

thing), so I decided that I would try and make friends with her at lunchtime. When Miss Hogan asked who would look after Kimi, I put up my hand. Not because I needed a new friend, but because I thought about how much I'd hate to be the new kid in the playground. We ate our lunch together and I asked if she wanted to swap my cheese stick for her packet of salt and vinegar chips. Turns out she loves cheese sticks (which I think are OK, but they're not my favourite) and I love salt and vinegar chips. She loves them too, but in the end I persuaded her that the cheese stick was much healthier for her.

Anyway, we started talking and soon found out that we had absolutely nothing in common. It was funny, but I still liked her anyway, even if she did rave on about her favourite singer and her great clothes and all sorts of boring girly stuff. In fact I liked her a lot, and I thought she'd be fun to have around. She knew everything about what was popular and trendy, and well, I knew everything about sport and stuff, so I thought together we'd make a good combination.

But then she went and mentioned there was this boy she'd like to meet. She was a fast mover for a second-grader. When she said his name was Andrew, my heart froze. My tongue got all thick and I started to sweat. Not *my* Andrew. How dare she?

I know you probably think I'm not the kind of girl who'd want to have a boyfriend, but you see I really like boys. They're much more fun to play with, and they have way better games. So when Kimi said that she thought Andrew was cute, I knew I had to set her straight immediately. I told her that he'd had the same girlfriend since kindergarten and that he wasn't interested in any other girls even if they did have long blonde hair and dimples. She glared at me suspiciously and asked how I knew all that. I told her that

I just did, and that if she knew what was good for her she'd stay away from Andrew, even though that was going to be difficult because I had planned for us all to play hand-ball together at lunchtime.

Luckily for me, big-mouth Rex started shouting, 'Snot loves Andrew, Snot loves Andrew.' I gave him my best evil stare (the one I learnt from Mum) and told him to shut up, but I think Kimi got the right idea about the two of us. From that day on she never mentioned that she liked Andrew, except just as a friend and good handball player.

As you might have guessed, 'Snot' is my nickname. I know it sounds gross, but it beats Pen or Nel or any of the other wussy names you can make out of Penelope. Mum thinks it's disgusting, but she respects my decision to let my friends call me by that name. I stress, though, that only my *closest* friends are allowed to use it. I told all the other kids I'd arrange for my Aunty Sandy's boyfriend Ozzie, who just happens to be a policeman and rides a big Harley Davidson, to pay them a visit if they dared call me Snot. To everyone else I am Penny or Scotty.

THE DOG

I have a dog called Roll Up. We call him Rolly for short. He's a golden retriever and Granddad says they are the best archaeologists in the world. I haven't worked out what he means yet, but he keeps on telling me that one day I'll understand.

Mum and Dad bought him for my

birthday this year. I thought it was really special that they got him together. For parents who are divorced they get on really well, which makes things a lot easier. I didn't want to seem ungrateful, but at first I was a bit disappointed. You see I really wanted a bitza. You know, 'bitza this and bitza that'. One of the kids at school, Rex — the one with the big mouth — told me what happens to all the mongrel dogs that get taken to his dad's vet surgery by the local dog catcher. The thought of all those abandoned puppies being put to sleep makes me feel terrible. So when I asked Mum and Dad for a puppy, I told them that I wanted a bitza from the pound. Then, when this perfect golden retriever arrived, I just didn't have the heart to tell them he wasn't really what I was after.

Mum let me take him to school for show and tell. Then Rex blabbed that he was the mongrel that someone had left in a box outside his dad's surgery the week before. I felt much better knowing that he was actually a bitza golden retriever, and Mum and Dad had saved his life.

Anyway, we hadn't thought of a name for him yet, so Mr Maslin said we should have a competition to see who could come up with the best one. There were heaps of suggestions — Wags, Rosie, Choco, Bruiser, Sparky. By lunchtime, there were about twenty names on the board, but I still didn't think that any of them were just right. Then, at lunchtime he kind of named himself.

When we went outside, we found him with his head in Rex's school bag eating the contents of his lunchbox. He'd already munched through a Vegemite sandwich (including the plastic wrap), some Tiny Teddies, and was halfway through a raspberry Roll Up. It was still hanging out of his mouth. So that's what we called him. I was pretty worried about the plastic wrap — you know, I thought it might get all tied around his intestines, but Rex said that he'd just poop it out later on. Everyone thought that was really gross, but I for one was glad to hear that the little guy wouldn't have to have open-gut surgery.

I was relieved too, because Mum said she couldn't afford dog food *and* vet bills. When we got home I made sure that I checked all his poos until I saw the evidence. It took him two whole days to get rid of it. Anyway, it must have been good for him really, because after that he could eat any-thing and he never got sick. He's my best friend, apart from Kimi and Andrew.

I used to try and sneak him into my bedroom at night, but one time when he was lying on the floor at the end of my bed, he barked and Mum thought I'd caught whoop-ing cough. She came running into my room, tripped over him and bashed her leg on the side of my bed. She even cried it hurt so much. I felt really bad, mostly because she didn't even chuck a mental at me because she was too busy bawling. I quickly took Rolly outside and told him off for sneaking in when I was asleep and almost killing Mum. I think she suspected that I had let him in, but from then on I decided that for Mum's health, I'd better make him sleep in his kennel. She had this enormous bruise on her leg and well, if she was ever going to get a new boyfriend, she couldn't go around with legs like an eighty year old.

THE BOYFRIEND

I suppose it sounds funny talking about your mum having a boyfriend. At first I thought I'd hate it if she ever went out with anyone, but then after Dad had been gone for over a year, I started to realise that Mum hardly ever smiled any more. When she played with us we made her laugh, especially when we played this game called 'Grandma's Undies'. You have to ask questions and the only answer allowed is 'Grandma's Undies'. At first Mum thought it was really disgusting. She did her best 'I'm a grown-up and you kids shouldn't play revolting games like that' routine. But then after Matt and I played it for about five minutes, she started to laugh, and after another couple of questions she had tears rolling down her cheeks. So now she is the best player, but only at asking the questions. She can never keep a straight face when we ask her. Especially ones like, 'What's that you're wearing on your head, Mum?' and 'Guess what we put up the flagpole at school today?' You get the picture?

But apart from when we were being silly with her, she didn't seem to smile very much. I was worried about her. After all, she was getting on a bit, and I didn't want her to be alone for the rest of her life, especially not after Matt and I leave home. I always hoped that Matt would leave home at a very young age, and although he always threatened to go, he never did. I think the doctor guy that he saw said that he was attention seeking to make up for feeling abandoned. At least that's what I overheard Mum telling Aunty Sandy. The doctor told Mum not to give in to him, and especially not to feel guilty. But I think she did anyway. Most of the time Matt got his own way and Mum always gave him lots of cuddles, and told him that she loved him.

Sometimes I wanted to explode and tell him to grow up and get over himself, but then I remembered this episode of Oprah that I watched when I was sent home from school with nits. Mum put this special foam treatment on my hair, which you had to leave in for an hour, so I asked her if I could watch a video while I waited for the critters to cark it. When I turned on the TV, this Dr Phil guy was talking about kids just like us. He said that often the child who was dealing better with the split got really annoyed with the other kids, and that the parents should help the kid who was OK to be more understanding of their siblings. I had to look up siblings in the dictionary. It took me a while, but I found out that it's just a fancy word for brothers and sisters.

So anyway, I decided that I would try really hard to be a better sibling, and not get annoyed with Matt when he was being all thingy about the divorce. Then Mum came in and yelled at me for watching 'inappropriate television' — her words, not mine! She made me watch *Anastasia* — I ask you, how old does she think I am? But when she left the room I turned Oprah back on. I thought it was really interesting. They were also talking about how lonely single parents can get and how they need adult company. It got me thinking about my mum and how sad she was. I thought maybe I could help her, so I asked Kimi and Andrew for some advice. That was when we came up with the plan.

THE PLAN

It was a simple enough idea. I was going to make it my mission to find Mum a boyfriend. That meant tracking down every single man in Dolphin Shores — no, I don't mean every single man, I mean every man without a partner. Well, the ones over thirty-five that is — I didn't think it would be very 'appropriate' for Mum to have a toy boy. Oh, and he had to be handsome, athletic, wealthy, like kids and hopefully not already have any brats of his own. I didn't like the idea of having a Brady Bunch family.

Kimi and Andrew thought it was a great idea. Andrew said that his dad and my mum would make a beautiful couple, but I pointed out to him that it might be a bit difficult seeing as though his parents were still happily married, and his mum was seven months pregnant. He saw my point.

Anyway, we agreed that if this plan was going to work, we'd have to put quite a bit of time into it. So we decided to meet at my place in the treehouse after school to work out the details. Oh, and we had to keep it quiet. If Matt found out, he'd blab to Mum and we'd all be in big trouble. Especially me, because as usual I was the brains of the operation.

So Kimi and Andrew came over straight after school. I told Mum we had this big

homework assignment and that we'd probably have to work on it every afternoon for at
least a week. Of course she wanted to know
what it was about, so she could help. I told
her it was on families. I wasn't really lying.
We were working on families. I just didn't tell
her it was about adding to ours. She got all
excited and said she'd dig out a whole lot of
old photographs and the family tree, *blah,
blah, blah*.

'That's great, Mum,' I told her, 'but Mr
Maslin says that we have to do all the work
ourselves this time. You know how much
trouble I got into last time when you helped
with my Captain Cook project.'

Mum looked at me sadly and agreed
that she'd just get some information together.

After the last time, I made her promise
never to get too involved with my projects
again. You see, because Mum's a graphic artist
she sort of got carried away with all the head-
ings and illustrations. It was pretty obvious

after my 'still-life rhinoceros', the project wasn't all my own work. Mr Maslin even wrote on it, 'Well done, Mrs Scott. A most beautifully presented assignment. If you ever consider a career change, you have great potential in the area of book illustrating. The information was quite good too, Penny.' I was so embarrassed. Fancy Mr Maslin giving Mum a better comment than me!

I told Mum that she could help out by making us some pikelets for afternoon tea, and while she was at it she could rustle up some Milo as well. That'd keep her busy for a little while.

We climbed up into the treehouse. It always made me a little bit sad when I went up there, because Dad had built it for us the Christmas before he left. I had to be strong though and realise that life goes on. I had to do this for Mum. Without my help she could be destined for a life of loneliness. Besides, as much as I loved her, I didn't want to have to live at home for the rest of my life, just so I didn't feel guilty about leaving her on her own. The thought of us still playing Grandma's Undies when she was eighty-five, and wearing her own grandma's undies, just didn't seem that funny.

As usual, Kimi was dressed in the dumbest clothes for climbing into tree-houses. I made sure that Andrew went up first so that he didn't see Kimi's knickers as she climbed up in her dress. At times that girl makes me so mad. She's just such a — a — a *girl*! I asked her why couldn't she wear board-ies like the rest of us, and she said they were scratchy and she didn't like the material. Yeah, whatever!

I took up my special notebook, the one with pandas on the front, to make sure that all ideas were written down. I decided to make Kimi the note-taker as she has by far the neatest handwriting. She got her pen licence when we were in Year 3. Mr Maslin said that I'd be lucky to have one by the time I went to university. But that's OK because I'm planning on becoming a doctor anyway, and everyone knows that they have the worst handwriting on the planet.

Andrew is definitely our ideas man. He's always coming up with really cool new games at school. He even invented a different version of Grandma's Undies, called Sausages. We played it at camp, because Mr Maslin said that Grandma's Undies was a bit too gross.

Andrew is really good at sports too. He's in the town soccer and tee-ball teams as well as doing Nippers and swimming training. That means he gets to hang out with lots of guys who might be just right for my mum. As well, his dad is a builder and they always have tradesmen hanging around at their place. At first I did think that maybe Mum was too good for someone like a plumber, but then I remembered Kimi's dad is a plumber and he's a really great bloke. I suppose I didn't want to set my standards too high. As far as I can tell there aren't too many stockbrokers or high-flying executives living in Dolphin Snores.

So, at exactly four o'clock on Monday afternoon, I called the first meeting of Plan FMAB (Find Mum a Boyfriend) to order. I suppose you might be wondering how a ten year old knows all about how to run a proper meeting. Well, my mum is the secretary of the Dolphin Shores Tennis Club. I picked up lots of special meeting words, like 'annual general meeting' and 'nominations' from her talking about it at home. I thought if we were going to make this plan work, we should follow some strict guidelines. That meant everything by the book. Well, as much as I could remember.

fMaB

I called the meeting to order. That wasn't really difficult seeing as though there were only three of us. Then I thought if we were going to be like a proper club we should think up a cool name, and have votes to be president and secretary and treasurer. Andrew said that was stupid because Kimi was already the secretary, and I was the boss, and he was the only one any good with money. I began to protest, but then he pointed out that he was the only one of us in the extension maths group, so I reluctantly saw his point. I hate it when boys are right. Anyway, we all agreed about the jobs we would do, but I couldn't see that Andrew was going to be very busy looking after the money — since we didn't have any.

We did agree that FMAB was a stupid name. We needed something much more exciting. Andrew suggested that we should call the plan 'Code Name something'. Kimi said we should call it 'Operation something', which I told her sounded a bit over the top. We weren't planning an air raid or starting a war.

'All right, Andrew, your idea is OK, but we have to think of what the code name is,' I told him.

We all sat there for ages, and nobody

could come up with anything good. Kimi said, 'Code Name Boyfriend' (der — that was stating the obvious); Andrew thought 'Code Name Partner'; and all I could come up with was 'Code Name New Guy'. They were all pretty dumb. Then Mum came clattering out the back door with our afternoon tea.

'Oh, hello, Mr Wright. Beautiful afternoon, isn't it?' she called to our elderly neighbour, who was pruning the roses on the fence.

'Lovely day indeed, Francine. Nice to see the kids up there in the treehouse. You know when I was a boy ...' Mr Wright began.

That was it!

'How about Code Name Mr Wright, but spelt r-i-g-h-t, not like Mr Wright next door?' I asked eagerly.

The others nodded. It was good. Kimi said that if Mum saw anything by accident, we could tell her that we were also doing a special project on oldies who'd fought in the war, and that Mr Wright was one of our subjects. She said I could tell Mum that she was a really bad speller.

Poor Mum. I could tell that she was stuck with Mr Wright by the way she was saying, 'Mmm,' and 'Ahhh yes, I see.' She was being polite because once Mr Wright started talking, it was almost impossible to get away.

'Sorry, Mr Wright. I'll have to go and give the kids their afternoon tea. I'm sure they're all starving, and the pikelets will be getting cold,' she said, trying to make her escape.

'No my dear, that's quite all right,' he replied. 'Wouldn't want them to expire now, would we? Off you go and we'll continue our chat another time.'

We could almost hear Mum's sigh of relief as she trekked down the yard to the bottom of the tree. Roll Up was dancing around her feet. He could smell the pikelets and was trying hard to get her to give him one.

'Would you kids like something to eat?' she called up to us. 'If you say you're not hungry, consider yourselves all DM.'

DM stands for Dead Meat. It's one of Mum's favourite expressions. She's always telling Matt and me that we'll be DM if we don't do this or that. Fortunately, we know she's just joking. I'm really glad I have a cool mum who says funny things. I always feel sorry for the kids at school whose parents are old and crusty.

There's this one kid in our class called Bronwyn, and her mum looks like she's about a hundred. Well, maybe that's exaggerating a little bit. She wears skirts with flowers on them, and always ties her grey hair back in a bun. I put my foot in it big time one day, when I asked Bronwyn if her grandma was picking her up from school. Well, I didn't realise it was her mum. She got all huffy and said that her grandma had passed away three years ago, thank you very much. I felt really bad and I tried to tell her too, but she wouldn't listen. I think she must have told her mum though, because Mrs Thompson has started wearing trousers, and it looks like she's put a colour in her hair. But they always stare at me when I try to be friendly. Oh well, their loss!

Afternoon tea was delicious. My mum makes the best pikelets in the universe, really fluffy with heaps of butter and jam — who worries about cholesterol when you're ten and a half? So we stuffed our faces and started thinking about how to find Mum her very own Mr Right.

Mr right?

First of all I thought we should write down a list of desirable characteristics. It took Kimi three goes before she was happy with the spelling of 'characteristics'. I told her to hurry up and just write 'good points'. She's such a perfectionist.

Top of the list he had to like kids. I said

that I'd prefer if he didn't already have any. I couldn't imagine suddenly having a couple of step-brothers and sisters. It was bad enough having to put up with one brother (with major psychological problems). Then Andrew said that he should be good looking too. He said that my mum was a real babe (his dad said so too), so she should go out with someone who looks half decent. Kimi thought a good head of hair always helped. I told her to write 'No bald blokes'. We started to giggle. Andrew said we should put 'No crome domes'. Then Kimi went all quiet and said she didn't think that was very funny. Andrew and I looked at her and shook our heads.

'But you were the one who said that he should have hair,' I said.

'Yeah, and then I remembered that my dad's almost bald, but he's still a cool guy,' she replied.

We said to take off the bit about the

hair. I suppose if he had everything else going for him we could overlook that point, but I insisted that we would never consider anyone with a comb-over. I still have nightmares about my mum's uncle, who has the worst one ever. You know what I'm talking about — when men start to go bald and grow the side bits really long, and then comb it over the top and slick it down with hair oil. Uncle Albert, Granddad's brother, has the comb-over to beat all comb-overs. Sometimes when we go out fishing with him and we're flying along in Granddad's tinny, all of a sudden these long strands of hair flick over and he looks like some weird old hippy. I suppose it is pretty funny even though it's tragic. Mum reckons Uncle Albert used to have lovely hair, and he probably just can't bear the thought of losing it all. He'd look a million times better with a number one all over, though, like Granddad.

But back to the list. Whoever we picked

had to be funny and have a good job. He didn't have to be a brain surgeon, but he had to have a career. We all agreed that was important. Then Andrew suggested that he should drive a really cool car, like a convertible.

'Yeah, and I suppose he should play cricket for Australia, have a speedboat and be a millionaire too?' I asked sarcastically.

Andrew nodded, so I punched him on the arm.

'Get real, Andrew. When was the last time you saw a good-looking millionaire bachelor in Dolphin Snores?' I pulled a face.

'Well, I just thought it would be cool, that's all. You didn't have to hit me,' he growled.

'Sorry,' I said in my huffiest voice. This was all getting much harder than I thought it would be.

We finally finished the list. It was two whole pages. I let Andrew keep the bit about the cool car just to keep him happy. Then again, when I thought about it, I wouldn't really mind if he did have a cool car. All the kids at school would be really jealous and *mmm* ... I could be driven to school in it, and everyone would look at me, and ...

'Snot, what's the next heading?' Kimi asked.

I jolted back to reality. 'Sorry, what was that?'

'The next heading. What is it? I hope it's not as hard to spell as "characteristics",' Kimi moaned.

'Sorry, I was just daydreaming.'

'Yeah, obviously,' Andrew quipped.

I ignored him. 'The next thing we need to think about is how to find someone with all these char-ac-ter-is-tics,' I said really slowly in syllables. 'I mean, we can't just put an ad in the paper, can we?' I asked no one in particular.

'Hey, that's not such a stupid idea,

Snot. Why *couldn't* we put an ad in the paper? We'd just have to get the replies sent to somebody else's place,' said Andrew excitedly.

'Yeah, right. And who would pay for this ad? And what would we say, anyway? "Wanted: one good-looking rich bachelor with trendy sports car and no kids for lonely mother of two"?' I must have been getting tired because my patience for dumb ideas had gone right out the window.

'Forget it,' he said. 'I was just trying to help. All right, Miss Smarty-Pants, you come up with something better.'

I racked my brain, but I couldn't think of anything. 'We could start our own intro-duction agency, so there, that's an idea,' I hissed.

'Pretty dumb one,' said Andrew. 'Like where are we gonna get the money for that?'

'Come on, you two, stop arguing,' begged Kimi. 'Think up some more things and I'll just scribble them down. Like when Mr Maslin gives us a new topic and we do that brainstorming thing on the board.'

'What about a survey? We could make up a survey and pretend we were doing a maths project and suss out which kids have parents who are divorced or separated. That might work,' Andrew suggested.

'I suppose it might,' I said reluctantly, 'but I don't really want any *step-siblings* from our school. Hey, what about sending love letters and saying they're from my mum?'

'Yeah, but who will we send them to?' asked Kimi. 'First of all we need a list of single guys. We can't just send love letters to men all over town.'

'Let's make a *lu-u-u-rve* potion,' Andrew cooed. 'They used to do that in the olden days.'

'You've been watching too many old movies,' I snapped. 'That sort of thing would never work. Besides, we haven't got a book of spells or anything. We'd probably poison the poor guy.'

'All right then, you think of something. All you ever do is say that my ideas are stupid. I'd like to see you do better,' Andrew snapped.

I gave Andrew my best evil stare. This wasn't working. All we were doing was getting on each other's nerves. I was beginning to think this was a really bad idea and we should just forget the whole thing.

Then suddenly I had a vision of Mum and me in terry-towelling dressing gowns and Tweety Bird slippers, sitting on the back verandah with our knitting, drinking sweet cups of tea and talking about the good old days when we played Grandma's Undies together. Erk, it was just too tragic. Something had to be done.

'All right, what have we got so far?' I asked Kimi.

She read out the notes she'd written.

None of the ideas sounded very good.

'Oh, come on. We're sitting here like a bunch of der-brains. We're smart, aren't we? We should be able to think of something,' I begged.

Andrew gave me a blank look and made his eyes go all big and shaky. Then out of nowhere he said, 'I'm going home.'

'Why, what's wrong with you?'

'There's nothing wrong with me. It's you, Snot. You're in a really bad mood, and I don't feel like hanging around with you if you're going to be so mean.'

'Well, go then. See if I care. Kimi and I don't need your help anyway,' I spat.

Then to my surprise, Andrew stood up and walked over to the ladder. I couldn't believe it. He really was going home.

'Where are you going?' I demanded.

'I told you, you're in a foul mood, you're mean and you're bossy, and I don't need to put up with you. I'm going home to do something fun — like my maths home-work. It'll be much better than sitting here listening to you bite my head off,' Andrew said as he disappeared down the ladder.

'So go!' I called after him.

I was dumbfounded. I sat there with my mouth open like a hungry Venus flytrap. We'd never had a real fight before. I couldn't believe he'd actually gone.

Then Kimi stood up and said she had to go too. Something about her mother needing help with the dinner. I knew she was lying, because her mum is one of those super-organised women who usually has meals prepared two days in advance. She's like the queen of the *Women's Weekly Menu Planner*. It's not like at our place, where we usually have a vote about half-an-hour before dinner time about what we want to eat. Matt and I always vote for pizza or hamburgers, but Mum says that since she's the only parent, she has the casting vote. She always wins, except on Saturday nights when she can't be bothered to cook.

We usually have pizza on Saturday night. Mr Giovani at the local pizza place knows us by name, and we never have to say what we want. Oh, except for one time when Mum said that she felt like a change, and instead of ham and pineapple she ordered a supreme. Mr Giovani thought it was a mistake, so he sent a ham and pineapple pizza along as well, just to be sure. His son Guido, who does the deliveries, said that his big brother Enzo got a clip around the ears for not taking our order properly. Mr Giovani wouldn't believe Enzo when he said that Mum had ordered something different. So just to keep the Giovani family peace we always stuck to the same thing from then on.

Kimi got up to leave and handed me my panda notebook. I asked if she could come over tomorrow to help and she made some lame excuse about having to go to the dentist. As if, I thought. She climbed down the ladder, yelled goodbye to Mum and thanked her for the pikelets. She called out to say goodbye to me but I pretended I didn't hear her. Then as she was going through the back gate I stood up and poked out my tongue. I thought it must have started raining because I felt something wet drop onto my t-shirt. Then I realised it was a tear. I could hardly believe that I was doing it. I never do it, never ever. Well, hardly ever, not even when Mum and Dad split up. I was crying.

THE STANDOFF

I stayed up in the treehouse for ages feeling sorry for myself. Who needed them anyway? I could do this on my own. How hard could it be to find Mum a boyfriend?

Rolly was at the bottom of the ladder whimpering. I threw a leftover pikelet down for him. It bounced off his nose and into the dirt. He wolfed it down anyway. That kept him quiet for about thirty seconds and then he started whingeing again.

'Shut up, Rolly,' I snapped, 'just go away.' He looked up at me with those big brown puppy-dog eyes and cocked his head to one side. There's no way I can stay mad at him when he does that. He's just too cute.

'I'm sorry, boy. I didn't mean it. I'll come down and give you a cuddle.'

As I scampered down the ladder, Mum yelled out to hurry up and come inside. Trouble was, I didn't feel like going in just yet. I was having a really good sulk, and I knew it.

'I'll be there in a minute.' I gave Rolly a big squeeze, and he playfully licked me on the cheek. 'Yuck, dog slobber — you have to learn not to do that, Rolly. Your breath is getting as bad as Snugglepuss, and hers is totally disgusting.'

Snugglepuss is Kimi's geriatric tabby cat. She only ever eats fish and at twelve years of age, after about a million sardines, she stinks. You'd think that some clever vet could make a fortune developing special toothpaste for cats and dogs. I might suggest that to Rex.

There I was thinking about Kimi again. I had to put her and Andrew right out of my head. If they weren't going to help, then I would just have to come up with some ideas of my own. After all, it was my mum who needed the boyfriend, so why should they care?

I picked up Rolly's dish and took it inside to get his dinner.

'Is everything OK, Penny?' Mum looked at me with her best 007 look — the one where she raises her left eyebrow and glares.

'I hope you didn't have a fight or anything?' she quizzed. 'Andrew and Kimi don't usually go home so early.' Boy, she was good

— I wonder if all parents have built in radar intelligence systems.

'Everything's fine,' I lied. I can't believe how clever parents are at sussing out when kids are fighting. But this time there was absolutely no reason to worry her with my dramas. If I told half the story, knowing her, she'd somehow manage to get me to spill the beans on what we were really doing, and then well, that would spoil everything.

If Mum knew that I was on a mission to find her a new partner she'd probably pack me off to boarding school, like she always threatens to do whenever Matt and I are fighting. It never worries me though, because Dad went to boarding school and he hated it, so he said that he would never make his kids go — not unless they really wanted to. I'm always trying to convince Matt that he would love boarding school. It would mean that he wouldn't have to see Mel any more on the weekends, or put up with me. But he once said Tim Bryson, one of the boys in his class, said they feed you liver and make you walk around with your underpants on your head for an initiation. Tim's brother Steven goes to boarding school up the coast. I told Matt that Tim was just making up stories to scare him, but secretly I didn't like the sound of it either.

Roll Up was jumping all over the back verandah waiting for me to return with his dinner. I was really fussy about his diet — even though he didn't share my concern, and ate anything that came within reach. His dinner was made up of puppy food with grated carrot and this special vitamin powder. Mum told me that when I got sick of mixing this concoction every day, Rolly would probably be just as happy to eat tinned food. I'm sure he would have been, but I was determined to be a model puppy parent.

At dinner, Mum asked me again if there was anything wrong.

'You're very quiet, Penny. Are you sure there's nothing the matter?'

'No, Mum. I'm OK — just a bit tired. Maybe I'll go to bed early.'

'OK, sweetie, but you would tell me if there was anything wrong?'

'Of course, Mum.'

I asked if I could be excused, and Mum said that I should go and have a bath and hop into bed. Matt could help with the washing up. Sucked in, I thought. He must have read my mind.

'Thanks, Snot — you can take the garbage out tomorrow night instead,' he growled.

'Matthew, be nice to your sister for a change. If she's not feeling well it won't hurt for you to do the washing up and take the garbage out.'

I smiled my best 'double sucked in' smile at him and went to run the bath.

I always find it especially relaxing after a long day to take a great big bubble bath —

as full as I can get it without slopping water all over the floor — well, not much water on the floor. As I lay there in the foam I started thinking about the plan. I really didn't mind the idea of writing a love letter — that sounded OK. But I'd have to type it up on the computer when nobody was around. And I still didn't have anyone to send it to. The next afternoon was soccer training, so no time then.

Suddenly, like a bolt of lightning, I remembered that the week before, Mum and Mr Maslin were having this really secretive conversation after the game. When I asked her what they were talking about, she said that it didn't matter and that it was one of those 'need to know' things, and at the moment I didn't need to know.

Maybe they liked each other. They were always laughing and joking around after training. Maybe that was it — Mum and Mr Maslin. After all, he did write a nice comment to Mum on my project. All I needed to do was help things move along a bit. Maybe if I wrote a love letter to Mr Maslin from Mum, then he would ask her out. I really liked him — he's a great guy, and he never talked about being married or having a girl-friend or anything.

'Are you ever getting out of the bath?' Matt yelled, and then burst in. 'Hurry up, Snot — you're not the only person in this family.'

'Get out, Maggot. *Muuum!* Matt's in the bathroom.'

I was trying to place the last of the bubbles over me so that Matt wouldn't see me naked. He has no respect for my privacy. I mean, I'm not a baby any more — and although there's still nothing to see, I hate it when he just barges in.

'You're sick, Snot — I'm not looking at you. Besides there's nothing to look at anyway.' He laughed.

I threw the plastic jug Mum uses to get the shampoo out of my hair at him, and he ran out slamming the door. Honestly, that boy has no idea about anything.

THE LOVE LETTER

That night under torchlight I wrote the love letter. It was pretty difficult holding the torch and writing under the doona at the same time. I made sure that Mum thought I was asleep before I started. The hardest part was not making it sound too mushy, and there was another problem too. I wasn't absolutely sure about Mr Maslin's first name. I had an idea that it was Paul. Anyway, after five drafts, I could hardly keep my eyes open.

I was planning on getting up really early and typing it out. I usually take Roll Up for a walk before school but I could ask Mum to take him instead, and tell her that I had to write a letter for English that I'd forgotten about. That way she'd be out of the house. I wasn't worried about Matt seeing it, because he never gets up until Mum practically drags him out of bed about ten minutes before we have to leave for school.

I set the alarm for six o'clock. I must have been in a really deep sleep, having one of my usual weirdo dreams, when suddenly I was aware that the radio was on. Rolling over, I hit the snooze button and something pointy stabbed me in the stomach. It was the pen. Then I realised why I had to get up. If I was going to type this love letter, I had to do it before Mum was out of bed, or if she was already up I had to convince her to take Rolly for a walk. I threw on my uniform and snuck out into the kitchen. There was no sign of Mum. I crept down the hallway to her bedroom.

'What are you doing up so early?' She was right behind me. I nearly jumped out of my skin.

'Nothing. It's just that I woke up and remembered I have to type up this letter for English, and it's due today. So I thought I'd get up and do it. You know how forgetful I am, and last night I went to bed so early,' I yawned.

'Well, you still look tired, sweetie. Why don't you show me what you have to do and I'll type it up for you. We can keep it a secret — after all, it's not a major assignment or anything. Mr Maslin doesn't have to know that I helped you,' she offered.

'No, no, it's fine, Mum. I have to

do it myself. I'll never improve my touch-typing if I don't practise. Besides, Mr Maslin would know that it wasn't my work, because your spacing and everything would be perfect.'

Now, there was a thought. If I typed it myself, he'd know that it was from a child. Maybe I should get Mum to do it. I could tell her that it was for this book we were reading, and we had to pretend to write a love letter from the main character to the guy she was secretly in love with.

'Um, Mum, maybe you could do it — just this once.'

'Sure, honey. Why don't you go and get it, and I'll turn the computer on.'

I quickly read the letter again — just to make sure that Mum wouldn't know what she was really typing. There was nothing to give it away. Paul could have been any old Paul, and F could stand for Francis or Felicity or Farrah. Now that was a good name. Why couldn't Mum have called me Farrah? Mum was in the study. I handed her the letter. She giggled when she read it.

> Dear Paul,
> I think you are so handsome. You are the loveliest person I have ever met.
> It would be great to get to know you better. I hope you feel the same.
> Love
> Your Secret Admirer
> F xxxxxxxxxx

'It's sweet, Penny, but maybe you could spice it up a bit,' she said.

'Oh, OK, Mum. What would you say?'

This was turning out even better than I'd hoped. Now Mum was writing the love letter herself.

'Well, I'd be a little more descriptive.'

She began typing. I was reading over her shoulder. It was fantastic.

Dearest Paul,
Your eyes are like shimmering
emeralds against a starry night sky.
Your hair is like the smoothest silk.
I long for you to hold me in your
strong arms and to have your soft
lips against mine.
I hope you feel the same.
My love always,
Your Secret Admirer
F xxxxxxxxx

'So what do you think, Pen? Is it too much?'

'No way, Mum. It's great. I'm sure Mr Maslin will love it.'

'Why would he love it? It's not for him — but maybe it could be? His name is Paul, after all,' she laughed.

'Really? I didn't know that.' I tried to play it cool.

I planned to leave the letter on his desk

that afternoon before we went to soccer then maybe afterwards he'd talk to Mum and things would happen. Honestly, this match-making stuff was all too easy. I didn't need Kimi and Andrew.

HUMILIATION

I left home to walk to school ten minutes earlier than usual. That way I could avoid meeting up with Kimi and Andrew. You see, we all live within a five-minute walk of school, and we usually go together. I heard Kimi call out to me when I was about to go in the gate, but I ignored her and went to put my bag down outside the classroom. I had the love letter safely inside an envelope with 'Paul' written inside a big love heart, on the front. It was a little bit wobbly, but I thought it didn't look too bad, considering my usual efforts.

Ignoring Andrew and Kimi, I went to see if I could play handball with Rex and his gang.

'Hi, can I play?' I asked.

'Yeah, OK, but what about Kimi and Andrew?' Rex asked.

'What about them?' I tried to look as if I couldn't care less.

'Oh, are you having a fight?'

'No, I just want to play with you guys instead. What are you anyway, the friend police? If you don't want me to play, I'll find someone else to hang around,' I replied.

'No, let her play, she's pretty good,' Joshua chipped in. 'You can be on my team, Snot, but we'd better win.'

'Oh, I see — no pressure on the new

girl,' I laughed, making sure that Kimi and Andrew could both see what a great time I was having without them. They walked over to the other handball court and started their own game. In a few minutes, they had heaps of kids coming up to ask if they could join in. I was doing my best to have fun, but to be honest, it just wasn't the same. I know I'm too proud for my own good, but I really wanted to show them that I was just fine without them.

All day I did my best to ignore both of them. It was hard during science because we're all in the same work group. I decided that if I had to talk it would be one word answers. Andrew wasn't talking to me anyway, but Kimi was trying to patch things up.

'Come on, you two — this is silly. Why are we fighting?' she begged. 'Snot, stop being so stubborn. This is just stupid.' She got angry and stormed off to plant her seeds in the Petri dish.

The rest of the lesson was dangerously quiet, and even Mr Maslin asked what was wrong with us, because we usually made more noise than the whole class put together.

Finally, Andrew broke the silence.

'So did you come up with any other plans?'

'What do you care?' I retaliated.

'I don't. But I just don't want you to make a fool of yourself by doing something totally stupid, that's all.'

'As if — give me some credit.'

'Have it your way, Snot. If you think you can manage this thing without us, then go right ahead.'

'I will. And thanks for your concern. It's touching,' I spat.

I was even more determined now to get the love letter to Mr Maslin. Right after school, I stole back into the classroom while he was on bus duty. His clipboard and whistle were there ready for him to collect before training, so I slipped the letter between the team list and the draw. That way he'd be sure to find it.

I was about to leave when Mr Maslin walked in.

'Hey, Penny, what's up?'

'Oh nothing, I just forgot my home-work sheet.'

'Well, you know you're not supposed to be in the classroom without a teacher. Why don't you go down to the field? I'll be there in a minute.'

'OK. I'll see you there. I'll get the balls from the sports room on the way.'

'Good idea. Thanks,' he replied.

I really wanted to hang around and see if he opened the envelope, but then he'd be suspicious. I ran down to the field, hoping like mad that it would all work out just the way I planned.

Training seemed to go for ages. My mind wasn't really on what I was doing, and

I made more mistakes than ever before. I even scored a goal for the other team when we had a game against the Year 6s. Everyone was giving me a hard time, but I barely noticed. I was watching the sideline to see if Mum turned up. She wasn't there — and then I remembered she was working late, and she said she'd see me at home after training. Bummer. Now Mr Maslin couldn't talk to her anyway.

Finally training was over and I was about to grab my bag and go home. There was no point in hanging around — nothing was going to happen now.

'Penny, can I talk to you for a second? I think there's something we need to clear up.'

'Sorry about that goal for the other team, Mr M. I'm just a bit tired, that's all. You know how it is after a long day at school,' I began.

'No, Penny, it's not about the goal. It's about this.'

He pulled the love letter out of his pocket.

'What?' I asked with my blankest look.

'I think you know what this is.'

'What, what are you talking about? I didn't write any love letter.'

Big mistake — I was a goner. He hadn't said that it was a love letter, but I just did.

'Ah-hah, and how did you know it was a love letter, Penny? I'm kind of gathering that your mum had some help with this. So what did you tell her? Was she writing another phantom assignment for you?'

'How did you know? What is it with mothers and teachers? Were you all born with the same radar intelligence systems, or do you have to go to university to get that?' I tried to make a joke to hide my complete embarrassment.

'Penny, I'm really flattered that you think I'd be a good match for your mum, but to tell you the truth I'm engaged. Your mum's a terrific lady, but we could only ever be friends.'

I was so humiliated. I wanted a giant hole to open up and swallow me, right there on the edge of the oval. It had all seemed so easy, and now I had made the biggest fool of myself ever. I hung my head and bit my quivering lip.

'Why, Penny? I don't understand why you think it's up to you to help find your mum a new partner. She's an attractive intelligent woman. There are lots of guys who'd love to take her out.'

'OK, so name one.' My voice wavered. I really didn't want to cry in front of Mr Maslin.

'Oh, Penny, it doesn't matter who. It was really sweet but I think you should forget about matchmaking and maybe concentrate on making sure that your friends are OK,' he advised. 'I think I'm right in saying there's a problem with you, Kimi and Andrew at the moment. The silence during science today was deafening. I could actually hear other groups working. It was a sure sign that all is not well in the Snot camp.'

'We just had a bit of a misunderstanding, that's all. We'll get over it.'

'Penny, your friends are really important, you know — far more important than trying to set your mum up on dates.'

I really didn't know what else to say. For once in my life I was totally lost for words.

'Now, do you think we could keep this a secret? I promise not to tell if you don't. And hey, if it doesn't work out with Joanne, I'll let you know,' he smiled. 'Just kidding!'

'Sorry, Mr Maslin. You must think I'm an idiot. It's just that you and Mum seem to get on so well, and when you were talking the other day and she wouldn't tell me what it was about, I thought maybe there was something going on.'

'We were talking about whether you should try out for the district soccer team, Pen. But after today, I think you'll need to pull out all stops next game — I wouldn't want to send along some kid who scores goals for the opposition,' he laughed. 'And I certainly don't think you're an idiot. Far from it, Penny. I think you're a great kid who just wants to see her mum happy. I hope when I have kids, they love me as much as you love your mum,' he replied.

I smiled. Mr Maslin really was a great guy. If I had to go and make a complete fool of myself, I'm glad I did it in front of him. At least I didn't have to worry that he'd go and tell the whole town about it.

I felt like such a moron. I thought I could do everything on my own. If Kimi and Andrew had been there, I bet one of them would have known that Mr M was getting married. Kimi would for sure — her mum knows everything that's going on in Dolphin

Snores. Then none of this would have happened. I'd stewed for long enough, and it was about time to set things right.

THE apOLOGY

I raced home thinking about Kimi and
Andrew. They were the best friends anyone
could ever want. And Andrew was so handsome and good at sport. All I could think
about was the way I'd behaved. What a cow.
Come to think of it, I'd have walked out on
me yesterday too, if I was them. I didn't know

why I'd been in such a bad mood. Maybe I was coming down with something. I once read in one of Mum's women's magazines that when kids are getting sick, they often get really short and snappy. Maybe I was getting the chicken pox or something. Then I remembered that I had them last year. It was totally disgusting. You almost couldn't put a pin between them. They were even up my nose and on my bottom. Just remembering made me squirm. Gross!

Maybe I was a totally nasty person and didn't deserve to have any friends. I didn't mean to be so bossy. I really wanted to make up. So I did the only thing a self-respecting ten and a half year old could do. As soon as I arrived home, I dumped my bag on the back step, grabbed Rolly's lead, and headed off to apologise.

'I'm just going to see Kimi and Andrew,' I yelled out to Mum as I went past the kitchen window.

'And hello to you too, Penny. How was your day? Great thanks, Mum, and how was yours? Did Mr Maslin like your love letter? Yes, it was wonderful. He thought it was fantastic,' she answered her own questions.

'Sorry, Mum. How was your day?' I asked.

'Fine, honey, but why do you need to go and see Kimi and Andrew? You were just at school together all day. Are you sure it can't wait until tomorrow?' Mum asked.

'No, I forgot something for my home-work, and I really need to see them *now*,' I shouted.

'Penny, did you have a fight or some-thing?' Mum asked.

Her antenna was on high beam again. She always knew when there was something up.

'No, well not really, but I just need to see them, OK? I promise I won't be long. Besides, Roll Up needs a walk. Please can I go? I'll be back in half an hour, and if I'm not I promise I'll do the washing up all week,' I pleaded.

'And you can take the garbage out too, Snotface,' Matt yelled from the verandah.

I poked my tongue out at him and made a face.

'You're already supposed to do the washing up all week,' Mum scowled. 'Oh, all right. Just as long as you're home by five-thirty. Go and do whatever it is you have to. And if you've been mean, young lady, make sure you sort it out. It's important to clear the air. You might like to use that word you find so hard to say to your brother. Starts with "s" ends with "y".'

Matt mouthed 'sorry' and pulled a screwy face back at me. He didn't think Mum was looking.

'Yes, Mum, I will. Oh, and thanks for being so cool. Be back soon,' I yelled as I unlatched the gate.

'And Matthew, you can come in here and help me with dinner.'

'But that's not fair. Why does she get to go and see her boyfriend and I have to peel potatoes? That sucks.'

'And you can watch your language, young man, or you'll be doing Penny's washing up duty too.'

I skipped out the gate smiling. It was great hearing Matt the Psycho getting into trouble. Served him right for being so mean to everyone else.

You'd think Roll Up hadn't been out for a month the way he bounded across the front lawn.

We ran down the street and around the corner to Kimi's place. Her dad was just arriving home from work.

'G'day, Mr Fletcher, big day at work?' I enquired.

'G'day yourself, Penny. What are you up to then?

'Oh, I just remembered that I needed to tell Kimi something for school tomorrow.'

'Go on in then, and could you tell Mrs Fletcher I'm home and I'm really thirsty,' he winked.

'Oh, I get you. I'll let her know,' I replied.

That was Mr Fletcher's not-so-subtle way of telling his wife to make sure she had a cold beer ready for him.

I knocked at the back door and went straight in. Seeing as though I spent about half my life at the Fletchers', I was long past the days of knocking and waiting to be asked in. I was practically family.

Mrs Fletcher was in the kitchen fussing over what smelt like another of her gourmet dinners. I used to love it when she asked me to stay for tea, but I've been a bit reluctant since the time she experimented with kangaroo stew. She didn't tell us what it was until afterwards. Although it tasted pretty good, I felt a bit funny about eating one of our national symbols.

Kimi's baby sister, Tiffani, was sitting in the high chair banging her spoon on the table and demanding her custard.

'Hi, Mrs Fletcher,' I said. 'Is Kimi here? I just need to tell her something. Oh, and Mr F is home and he said to tell you that he's really thirsty.'

'She's in her room, love,' said Mrs Fletcher. 'Can you do me a big favour, Penny? Could you grab a beer from the fridge for me? Tiffani's in such a bad mood today, if I don't hurry up and give her her custard, I'm afraid she'll start whingeing again and honestly I just don't think I could take any more.'

'Sure thing!' I grabbed the ice-cold can out of the fridge and put it on the kitchen bench.

'You're a sweetheart, Penny. Kimi's lucky to have a friend like you,' Mrs Fletcher smiled.

That made me feel even worse. If only she knew what a cow I'd been the past couple of days. Anyway, I headed off to find Kimi. She was in her bedroom with the door closed.

I knocked, and she asked who it was. Reluctantly, I said 'Snot,' and asked if I could come in. She didn't sound very enthusiastic.

'What are you doing here, Penelope?' she asked.

I blurted it all out straight away, about me being a bad-tempered cow and how I was really sorry and could she forgive me because she was my very best friend and without her and Andrew I was nothing. (Perhaps I was a little melodramatic, but I needed her to know exactly how sorry I was.)

At first Kimi didn't say anything. Then she grinned and said of course she'd forgive me, and that it wasn't really her that I'd upset.

'Sometimes you're a real pain,' she said,

'but at least you're not too proud to say sorry. I'll see you tomorrow.'

'And will you help me with the plan?' I begged.

'Of course I will. Who else is going to take notes if I don't? Nobody would be able to read your scrawl — not even you,' she smiled.

'Thanks, Kimi. See you tomorrow. I've got to run to see Andrew before my half-an-hour leave is up. If I'm late home, I told Mum I'd do the washing up for a week,' I said as I raced off down the hallway. 'Gotta go, Mrs F. See you later.'

I grabbed Rolly's lead, which I'd kind of tied, but not very well, to the back verandah post, and raced out through the back gate.

'See you, Mr Fletcher,' I called out.

'Bye, Scotty,' he yelled back.

I told Rolly that it was a race to see who was the fastest to Andrew's place. Luckily he only lived six houses away from Kimi. I ran around the back and left Rolly loose in the yard. He could keep Andrew's dog Bimbo company for a few minutes. Panting loudly, I knocked at the back door. Mrs MacDonald flung it open and asked me to come in. Andrew was in the lounge room watching TV. He looked surprised to see me.

'Andrew, I'm really sorry about everything. I was wrong and mean,' I blurted.

He seemed shocked. I suppose he didn't expect me to come over and grovel.

'I'm really sorry. I couldn't stand the thought of us not being friends and, well … say something would you?' I asked.

'Well, well, well,' he began. I could tell that he was going to enjoy watching me squirm. 'This is new. Penelope Estella Grace Scott apologising. I can see the headlines now. "Snot says sorry!"' he smirked.

'Well?' I looked at him again.

'Well what?' he asked.

'Do you accept my apology? Are we

friends again? Will you come over to help with the plan tomorrow? Do I have to get down on my hands and knees and beg? Do you really need to be this cruel?' I fired the words at him.

He really was enjoying this new found power. Even though we'd never had a proper fight before, Andrew was pretty right about the fact that I hardly ever admitted being wrong. But you know what, I felt good about it. I think I had learned a big lesson, and even though Andrew was now acting like a smug idiot, I didn't really care.

'Well?' I stared at him with one of my best evil stares. He stared back and we started a staring competition. Then I started to smile and he did too. We both cracked up laughing, and I pounced on him and tickled him until he begged for mercy. The old tickle treatment worked on him every time.

'Of course I forgive you, you idiot,' he laughed. 'Only, the next time you're so mean, don't expect to get off as easily. And hey, why did you suddenly come to your senses?'

'Let's just say that I realised today that my friends are more important to me than my pride,' I replied. 'So will you help me with the plan again? I think three heads are much better than one.'

'Did something happen, Snot?'

'No, not really. Well, yes, but I'll tell you about it when I get over the embarrassment, that's all.'

So now I could go home knowing that my two best friends didn't hate me, and that we could get stuck back into Code Name Mr Right — hopefully without me making a fool of myself again!

THE MESS

Andrew and I walked out the back so I could get Roll Up. I looked around the yard and was pleased to see that for once he'd behaved himself. It was always a risk leaving Rolly in someone else's yard. He had a real thing about destroying other people's property. I was relieved to see there was no shredded newspaper or upended garbage bins. My shoes were on the doormat. Better still, Andrew's brand new Nikes were still there too. I was just starting to feel really proud of him, when Andrew let out a horrified yell.

'Oh no! Rolly, Bimbo, what have you done?' he shouted.

'What, what are you on about?' I looked at him. 'There's no mess or anything. I'd say that for once Roll Up's been a model visitor.'

'Oh yeah, you think so. Look over the fence,' he said.

My jaw dropped. I couldn't believe what I was seeing. 'Oh no, they couldn't have,' I pleaded. But they could, and they had.

Then right on cue, Roll Up and Bimbo appeared from around the side of the neighbour's house, clutching part of the evidence in their mouths. Both of them were covered in mud from head to toe and looked as though they had half the botanical gardens stuck to their filthy backs.

You could almost see the two of them smiling, thinking about how much fun they'd just had. Not caring one bit about the chaos they'd caused.

This time Roll Up had gone too far. He never did anything naughty at home. He saved it all up for when I took him out (or when he escaped under the fence). But this time he'd really outdone himself. It was worse than when he brought home Mr Thomas's rubbish and left it strewn all over the front yard. Much worse than when he got out and chased Mrs Larkin's cat up a tree and we had to call the fire brigade to come and rescue it. It was even worse than when I took him to Kimi's and he chewed up her dad's favourite old slippers. Mr Fletcher was annoyed but Mrs Fletcher said that Rolly had done her a big favour — she'd been trying to get him to throw them out for years and now he had no more excuses.

At least before there'd been no real

permanent damage. But this time was different. I thought about pretending that he wasn't my dog, but everyone in Dolphin Shores knew Roll Up. Everyone stopped and gave him a pat. Mr Madden, the butcher, always saved him a bone. Problem was that everywhere I went, Rolly went too, so I couldn't really deny he was my dog.

'What are we going to do?' I was close to tears. 'We have to do something. We can't just pretend it didn't happen.'

Andrew called out to Bimbo and Roll Up. They both came racing home around through the back gate.

'I mustn't have closed the latch properly. I'm sorry,' I sighed.

Both dogs were still clutching part of the torn sheets in their mouths. I knew we'd have to go next door and see just how much of a mess they'd made. From Andrew's back verandah it didn't look good.

'Who are the new neighbours?' I asked.

'I don't know. I haven't met them yet. They only started moving in yesterday. But Mum said they spent heaps of money having the entire backyard landscaped after the Smiths moved out. Mum said she never thought a backyard could look so good. It's like a tropical paradise with a little lagoon pond and a waterfall and everything.'

I looked at Andrew. I could tell he was scared too.

'Come on,' I said. 'We'd better go and see exactly how much mess those two have made.'

Andrew and I opened the gate. Bimbo and Roll Up tried to follow us but we slammed it shut and I yelled at the pair of them to get back inside. Rolly looked guilty, but Bimbo just wagged her fluffy Maltese terrier tail. She sure had the right name.

There was no car in the driveway and we couldn't see any lights on, so Andrew and I walked around to the back of the house.

Rolly and Bimbo had obviously enjoyed themselves. They'd ripped the sheets off the clothes line, torn them to shreds and then dug up at least half the plants in the garden. Now I knew what Granddad had meant about golden retrievers and their archaeology skills — he was a champion excavator, that's for sure!

There were muddy paw prints leading into this little pavilion around the side of the house, and when we entered, Andrew and I both gasped in shock. A great big concrete statue of what looked like a Greek God was lying on the ground with its head broken off. It was worse than I imagined. The yard looked as though it had been stampeded by a herd of cattle. I could hardly believe that two dogs — one of them only half a dog really — could have made so much mess.

'What'll we do?' I looked at Andrew. 'It's awful. The neighbours will hate us. I don't think we can clean this mess up on our own.'

'All right, we'll have to go and tell Dad and maybe he'll help us,' Andrew said. 'He won't be happy. The Smiths didn't like us because we complained to the council about their greyhounds. I reckon Dad's pretty keen not to get offside with this lot. Come on.'

I'd always thought that the MacDonalds had every right to whinge about their old neighbours. The Smiths had kept sixteen noisy greyhounds that barked all the time, not to mention being disgustingly smelly.

We ran back over to Andrew's place. His dad was unloading tools from the back of his ute in the garage.

'What are you two up to, eh?' he asked.

rescue

We told him the whole gory story. When we took him next door, I thought he was going to have a heart attack.

'Good grief, those two hounds have been busy. You couldn't have been here for more than ten minutes, Penny. If it wasn't so awful I'd probably laugh. Come to think of it, I wish we had a video of the whole event. Things like this always get the big money on *Funniest Home Videos*.'

Plump tears began to roll down my cheeks.

'Come on, Penny. It's not that bad — nothing a bit of hard labour won't fix. The new people won't be back until the weekend, so we've got a few days to get it sorted. And then, Penny, I think you and Andrew should book those two dogs in for some training. Don't they have puppy school down at the vet's? Maybe we'll have to send young Rolly to the puppy juvenile detention centre — if he doesn't learn to behave himself, that is.'

'Thanks for being so great about all this, Mr Mac. I'm really sorry,' I snuffled.

'Don't worry, Penny. It'll be all right.'

I could tell that he was pretty annoyed, but he's such a good bloke he kept his cool and agreed to help us fix everything. Andrew was right about him not wanting to get off-side with the new people. Apparently his dad had already met them, and they weren't moving in properly until the following week-end. He said they seemed like a terrific pair. He was a doctor, taking over old Dr Barnes's surgery, and she was an interior designer. He said he didn't want a repeat of the fiasco with the Smiths. He reckoned things got so bad they had poisoned his lawn.

At least that meant we had a few days to try and get everything fixed. The sheets were going to be a problem. I only had $25 in my bank account, and Andrew said that he wasn't much better off. Mum was going to be really peeved about having to spend money on somebody else's sheets — especially when she was only saying the other day, how much she'd like to get some new bed linen for herself.

Mrs MacDonald came to the rescue there. She said she'd seen the exact same sheets on special, and she would get them for us and wash them and everything, ready for us to give to the neighbours on Saturday morning. She even said we could do jobs for her to pay them off, so I didn't have to ask Mum for the money. Her new baby was due soon and she said that I could be a very useful extra pair of hands. I was secretly hoping that it didn't mean any nappy duty. I could cope with the feeding and playing, but I didn't think I was ready to handle the poo patrol.

As for the statue, I didn't see how we could fix that. But Mr MacDonald said that he had some special epoxy (which is really strong glue), and that he'd have a go at sticking the head back on. I was really worried that it would look obvious — like a Frankenstein garden statue.

I felt really bad because I'm sure Roll Up was the ringleader. Bimbo just doesn't have the brains to do anything so stupid.

We had to put Code Name Mr Right on hold until after the weekend.

With Mr MacDonald's help we managed to replant everything and get the grass looking OK too. Even Kimi came to give us a hand. Not that she was very useful. It was tragic that at her age she was already worried about breaking a nail. Andrew and I got right into it. I like getting my hands dirty. But I screwed up my nose at spreading out the chook-poo. A girl has to have some standards!

Anyway, after three days the yard looked almost as good as before. The statue had its head on again and with a bit of grey paint, you could hardly see where the join was — unless you looked at it up close. I suggested that we should give it a necklace, but Kimi said that would only draw attention to things. It was lucky she was so cool at fashion.

Still the worst was yet to come. Mr

MacDonald and Mum both agreed that we had to go and tell the neighbours what had happened, and offer to mow their lawns for free for as long as they wanted. Andrew and I thought that was a bit rough, seeing as though we didn't actually make the mess ourselves. But Mum said that the dogs were our pets and we had to take responsibility for them.

Matt, my scumbag brother, thought the whole thing was hilarious and offered to come over and watch when we apologised. Andrew told him to go boil his head (he's so cute when he's angry and I love it when he tells Matt off). For moment I forgot that I was going to try and be a more understanding sibling and I told Matt to go back to the psycho doctor where he belonged. I instantly regretted saying that because Mum heard and said I couldn't watch TV for a week.

Sometimes when you're ten and a half, life is just not fair.

I wasn't looking forward to Saturday, but on the other hand I wanted it to hurry up and arrive so that we could get it over with. I never was very patient — especially with Matt.

saturday
too far away

On Saturday morning I walked over to
Andrew's — alone. Roll Up wasn't allowed
out of the yard unless he was being taken for
a walk, straight out and back again. I wasn't
supposed to stop anywhere in case he
decided to try his paws at landscaping
someone else's place.

Mrs MacDonald had washed and folded the sheets and tied them with a big pink ribbon. Andrew and I had to write them a welcome to the neighbourhood card. We both suggested that we could just write an apology, and leave it on the doormat with the sheets, but Mrs MacDonald shook her head.

We hung around out on the back verandah for ages. Even playing Grandma's Undies didn't cheer either of us up. Andrew asked, 'What's on the clothes line?' I answered, without even a hint of a smile, 'Grandma's Undies.' Neither of us laughed. We sat out there for ages until finally a car pulled into the driveway.

'Hey, cool car,' Andrew stared. 'I hope they forgive us. I wouldn't mind getting a ride in that.'

I had to admit it was a head turner. Red and racy — a two-door sports. The guy who got out wasn't bad either. The thought crossed my mind that it was a pity he was married. Andrew must have been thinking the same thing.

'Hey, Snot, he and your mum would make a good-looking couple,' he joked.

'Yeah, remember you said that about your dad and my mum too. It's just not going to happen.'

'Well, we'd better go. Grab the sheets, Andrew,' I instructed.

'Why do I have to carry them? It was your dumb dog who caused this mess in the first place,' he complained.

I was about to tell him off when suddenly I felt very guilty. He was right — again. I took the sheets and marched off through the side gate. If I had to do this, I was going to hold my head high and grovel my heart out. Mr Maslin always says that if you are going to do anything in life, you should always do your best. So I was about to do the most serious sucking-up in history.

ETHAN

I walked straight up to the front door and knocked loudly. Andrew, the wuss, was dragging his feet. 'Come on, hurry up,' I hissed.

'I'm coming. Get off my case, Snot,' he glared.

It seemed like we stood there for ages, me clutching the sheets and fiddling with the pink bow, and Andrew scraping his feet on the tiles. I was just about to knock again when the door opened. He was huge — at least six feet tall and handsome too, with a thick mop of blonde hair. I couldn't think of anything to say.

'Hello,' he said. 'Can I help you?'

'Umm, ahh, I'm Snot, I mean, Penny and this is Andrew. He lives next door.' I shifted from one foot to the other.

'Oh, hi there. I'm Ethan James. I guess we're going to be neighbours. Would you kids like to come in? I'm sorry I can't offer you anything to drink unless you like water. We've only just arrived, and Kate won't be here until tomorrow,' he said. 'I'm a bit low on supplies.'

We followed him inside. The house was almost unrecognisable. When the Smiths had lived there it was all dark and daggy. They had disgusting shag pile carpet and mirror tiles on the wall in the entry. Andrew and I must have looked shocked. Everything was all bright and trendy. They'd taken out some walls and the kitchen was like one in the magazines Mum bought.

'Wow, the house looks amazing,' Andrew gawped. 'I wouldn't have recognised it. Mind you, I didn't come over here very often before.'

He didn't think he should tell him that the last time he came over it was with his dad and Sergeant Maxwell, when his dad had accused Mr Smith of poisoning their lawn.

'Thanks, Andrew. Yeah, we like it. Kate's an interior designer. We didn't want to move in until everything was done, and the landscaping took forever,' he replied.

Then suddenly I remembered why we were there in the first place. I stared at Andrew and then looked at the sheets. It was obvious he wasn't about to say anything, so I thought I'd better.

'Umm, Mr James, we came over here to

give you these, and to apologise for the mess that our dogs made in your yard. But we've fixed it all up, and it looks as good as before, and Andrew's dad reckons the ferns have even grown since Wednesday,' I thrust the bundle into his hands.

'Sorry, what's this for?' he asked.

'Well, on Tuesday, I came over to see Andrew because ...' I started.

He interrupted and said that maybe we should go and sit down.

'Now slow down, Penny. I want you to explain exactly what happened,' he said kindly. 'And for goodness sake call me Ethan. Mr James is my dad and I'm Dr James anyway.'

It was awesome. Andrew and I told him everything, and he wasn't even mad. He laughed about some of it, and said he remembered when he was a kid, they had a dog called Susie, who was fond of gardening in other people's yards. He said his dad used to throw a gumboot at her as she raced in through the gate and down the backyard with her tail between her legs.

We could hardly believe how cool he was. He thanked us for the sheets and said that Kate would really appreciate that we replaced them. They were her old favourites. He said Kate had ordered him a new washing machine and it was the first thing that was delivered. She'd insisted on giving him a lesson and had brought the sheets over so they could give it a trial run. She'd hung them out and obviously forgotten to take them in before they'd left the previous Sunday.

When we told him about the statue, he said that we shouldn't have worried about gluing the head back on. Apparently, he can't stand it, and he only kept it because his mum made him feel guilty about it. It was one of those 'special' Christmas presents from his Aunt Gladys — you know, that you have to bring out every time the relatives come to visit. He'd tried to put it in an out of the way part of the garden, so he wouldn't have to remember to lug it out of the garage when she came over.

He asked us about school and stuff and said we were welcome to come around any time. He even said he'd like to meet the two hounds responsible. As we were leaving he said to tell Mr and Mrs MacDonald that he and Kate would come over and meet them properly on Sunday afternoon, once they'd got a bit more settled.

rELIEf

We walked back to Andrew's breathing a huge sigh of relief.

Andrew had offered to do the mowing, but Ethan said that he already had a guy lined up, and he didn't want the two of us chopping ourselves to bits on the mower. I suspect that he probably didn't trust us to do a good enough job, but at least he was too kind to say so.

Mrs MacDonald was standing in the kitchen making Mr Mac a cuppa.

'How did it go?' she enquired. 'I hope you two apologised loud and long.'

We told them all about it. She and Mr MacDonald said they were really proud of us both, and it was great that Dr James was such an understanding fellow. She made us some Milo and a sandwich.

'And he's a real hunk too,' I told Mrs MacDonald. 'Tall and good looking — a bit like a movie star.'

'You should see his car, Dad. It's a red sports,' Andrew added.

'Sounds like our new doctor has made a big impression,' said Mr Mac. 'Wonder what the wife's like?'

'Well, you'll find out tomorrow because Ethan said that they'd come over and say hello in the afternoon,' Andrew said.

'What's this "Ethan" business? Shouldn't you be calling him Dr James?' Mrs MacDonald asked.

'No, it's cool. He said to call him Ethan,' I told her.

I thought I'd better get going so I thanked Mrs MacDonald for lunch, and for fixing everything up with the sheets. I told her I'd be over to help her with the baby when it was born, which looking at the size of her stomach could have been any minute.

Andrew walked out the front with me and asked when we were going to work on Code Name Mr Right. I thought maybe we should start again the following week. I was a bit tired after all the events of the last few days. I was going home to veg out on the couch and watch movies with Mum. Hopefully Matt had gone over to one of his mate's places. I didn't feel like talking to him.

On the way home I was thinking about Ethan James. He was such a nice guy. He liked kids, he drove a great car and he had gorgeous hair and a good job. He was perfect — except for one thing. He was married, to Kate — the one with all the decorating talent. Oh well, there was no point thinking any more about it. He was unavailable, and we still had to come up with a plan to find Mum Mr Right.

GOOD NEWS

On Sunday night Andrew called. I was help-
ing Mum with the washing up. Matt
answered the phone and shouted, 'Hey,
Snotface, it's your boyfriend.'

I told him to shut up and grabbed the
phone. Andrew said he'd rung to tell me
some good news. He said that Ethan and

Kate had called over to their place that after-noon, and she was a real babe. Long blonde hair, tall and with perfect teeth. I wasn't the least bit impressed.

'So what — you've got the perfect couple, Ken and Barbie, living next door. All that's missing is the campervan and pink sports car. No wait, I guess you're about to tell me that she has the sports car.' I laughed at my own joke.

'No, der-brain,' he said. 'I didn't ring to show off. I wanted to let you know that they're not married.'

'Yeah, but they live together. So what? They might as well be married. Maybe they're engaged?' I replied.

'Wrong again. They look alike,' Andrew said.

'So, they say that people who look alike often fall in love. I don't understand why any of this is good news.' I was losing my patience.

'I suppose I'll have to spell it out for you then. They're not a couple. They're brother and sister,' he laughed.

'Brother and sister. So they're not together. You should have said so, you idiot.' My mind was racing. 'Hey, are you thinking what I'm thinking?' I asked.

'Sure am. I think Dr James and your mother would make a lovely couple. Oh, and I found out how old he is too. Thirty-eight. Kate's only going to live with him until she finishes the renovations on her own place. She's starting a business here in town. He's not married and never has been, and he doesn't have a girlfriend either.'

Andrew was a real treasure trove of information. I asked how he found out so much and he said that he just acted like a dumb kid until his mother started getting suspicious about all the questions he was asking. She told him to stop being rude and prying into other people's private lives.

Andrew told Ethan that he'd better get used to people sticking their noses into his business now that he lived in Dolphin Shores — the gossip capital of the coast. His mum said that wasn't true, and he had moved to a really lovely part of the world, where people just cared a lot about one another.

Anyway, this new information changed everything. We'd found Mr Right. Now we just had to work out a way of getting them together. At least we were halfway there. I could hardly wait to tell Kimi. I asked Mum if I could call her up, but she said I'd see her at school tomorrow. I couldn't wait that long. I was busting.

'Please, Mum. It's really important. I'll only be a couple of minutes. I promise,' I begged.

'Oh, all right. Honestly Penny, you never let up. Five minutes, then I'm coming in there to say goodbye for you,' she said.

I rang Kimi and she was as excited as

me. She'd seen Dr James in the newsagency with her mum that morning. He'd said hello and introduced himself. Kimi's mum even said he was so cute that she'd think about switching doctors.

I got off the phone before my time limit was up. I couldn't risk having Mum overhear any of our conversation.

As I drifted off to sleep, I imagined my mum and Ethan James. Happily married. Us living in his beautiful house — they'd have added a pool with a waterslide of course. Me, living next door to Andrew. Matt, gone to live with Dad — permanently. A perfect life.

THE CRISIS

I must have been in the middle of a lovely dream when something woke me up. There was the most awful noise coming from Matt's bedroom. I was half awake when I realised his light was on and Mum was racing around. Then I heard him vomit. Yuck, I hate the up-chucks. I rolled over and buried my head under the pillow. I hoped I wouldn't get it.

I tried to go back to sleep, but the noise was getting louder. He must have been feeling really gross. Matt was a lot of things, but not usually a whinger. I actually started feeling a bit sorry for him. Last time I had the vomits I threw up all over my bed. Too disgusting!

Then I realised Mum was on the phone. She sounded a bit frantic.

'He's got a fever, and he's been vomiting,' I heard her say. 'No, I can't drive him over because I haven't got a car,' she said.

I wondered what she was talking about — of course we had a car. Then I remembered that it was down at Maloney's garage being serviced. I sat up and started to feel a bit worried. Maybe Matt was really sick. Even though he was a first class pain in the butt most of his life, I suppose I didn't like the idea of anything really bad happening to him.

Mum sounded scared and upset. I got out of bed to see what was going on.

'What's wrong?' I found her in the kitchen.

'Look, your brother's really sick and the doctor who's on call is over at Crystal Bay. He won't be back for about two hours. Matt's in agony and I need to do something.' She sounded pretty desperate.

I racked my brain, then I thought about Dr Ethan James. Bingo!

'Mum, what about the new doctor? He lives next door to Andrew. Maybe we could get him to come,' I asked.

'I'm sure he won't be in the phone book yet. No, I'll try Dr Rodgers first. Then if I get desperate maybe we'll try him,' she replied.

No luck with Dr Rodgers either. His phone rang out so he must have been away or something.

'Probably on another golfing holi-day. Where are they when you really need

them?' Mum muttered. 'I have to do something. I've never seen Matt so sick. I'm afraid
it might be serious.' I could tell she was really
nervous.

Despite what I said before, there are
lots of good things about living in Dolphin
Shores, but medical treatment isn't one of
them. The nearest hospital is two hours
away, and even then it's not very big. Mum
looked in the phone book under 'James' —
there was no number listed. So, after Matt
had thrown up about ten more times, I
finally convinced her to call Andrew's mum
and see if she could get Dr James. Mum said
she felt awful calling Mrs MacDonald (in her
seven-and-a-half-month pregnant state) at
one o'clock in the morning. Then Matt let
out a terrible wail. Mum picked up the
phone and dialled, and spent the next five
minutes apologising to Mrs Mac for having
no other choice.

Mrs MacDonald was really great about

it. She said that Mr Mac was already on his way next door and that it was an emergency and Mum shouldn't worry. Besides, she hadn't really been asleep because the baby caused her to have such bad indigestion, she spent half her life in the kitchen drinking antacids.

About ten minutes later Mr MacDonald arrived at our place with gorgeous Dr Ethan James. Even at one o'clock in the morning Ethan was a hunk.

'Hi, Penny,' he said.

I said hi and asked how the garden looked. He laughed and said that everything was growing well.

'Now, where's this brother of yours?'

Mum was so grateful she gave Mr Mac a big hug. He and I went into the kitchen and Ethan and Mum went to see Matt.

After a few minutes they came back out and Ethan called Child Flight to take Matt to hospital in the city. It seemed my boofhead brother had a really serious appendicitis. I was insanely jealous that he was going to get a ride in a helicopter, but then on the other hand I was glad it wasn't me who had to have an operation at the end of the trip. Mum arranged for me to go and stay the night at Andrew's. Ethan bundled Matt into Mr MacDonald's car and we drove off to the footy field to wait for the helicopter. It was the only place it could land. Matt was looking pretty green.

'Penny, I thought you told me that nothing exciting ever happens in Dolphin Shores. Since I've been here there's been action aplenty,' Ethan joked.

We waited about ten minutes and saw the spotlight from the helicopter in the distance. Sergeant Maxwell came down to the field to make sure everything was OK. Apparently they always alert the local police when they have to land in a public place. I suppose it can get tricky if they have to come in on a Sunday afternoon in the middle of a footy game.

Matt looked really awful. I said goodbye and gave him a hug. I don't know what came over me, but he sort of half smiled.

'So you do love me?' he said.

'Get real, Matt. I just don't want you to be sick because it upsets Mum.' I turned away quickly. There was no way I wanted him to see me crying. Then I realised for someone who hardly ever does that, boy, I'd been turning on the waterworks a lot lately.

I said goodbye to Mum and gave her a tight squeeze.

'It'll be OK. Ethan will look after him.' I tried to reassure her — and me at the same time.

'I know, sweetie. Now you be good for Mr MacDonald. I'll call you in the morning.'

And with that, they loaded Matt into the helicopter, and he, Mum and Ethan flew off into the night. Mr MacDonald and I drove back to their place. He told me not to worry — Matt was in good hands.

I wasn't that scared any more. I suppose I was secretly hoping that Mum and Ethan got on OK. I was a bit upset though — she wasn't exactly looking her best. She'd thrown on her tracky-dacks and scraped her hair back into a ponytail, but she was too worried even to put on any lipstick. Not at all like my mum. Usually she looks fantastic. Sometimes I find it hard to believe we are even related. I hate having to get dressed up. Last time we had our school photos, Mr Maslin said that all the girls had to wear their dresses, not shorts. I told him I didn't want to wear a dress and that he could just tell the photographers I was a boy. Mum wasn't the least impressed, so I had to wear the ugly sack of a thing.

I finally got to sleep, and then it seemed like about five minutes later it was morning. Andrew had slept through the whole drama, so he was a bit surprised to see me in the spare room.

Mum rang and said that Matt had had the operation and was going to be fine. She had to stay with him for a couple of days, and Dad was going to drive up to see them and take her some clothes. It was all arranged for me to stay at Andrew's until she got back. Mr MacDonald had a key to our place, so we would go over later and get me some clothes. Mum asked if I could go over every afternoon, feed Rolly and take him for a walk. Mr Mac said that he could come and stay at their place, but Mum said she felt better if he was left at home. She was worried about him teaching Bimbo more bad habits.

Mum said that if it was all right with the MacDonalds, maybe I could stay home from school that day and give Mrs MacDonald a hand around the house. She thought I might be too tired for school. Andrew begged to be allowed to stay home too, but his mum said she was quite looking forward to having a day with me on my own. We were going to play ladies, and she said we could even go out for coffee. Andrew moaned and whined, but he still had to go. It was a bit strange seeing him leave for school and me staying at home with his mum. I think Mrs MacDonald was hoping that the baby was a girl, so she was going to get in some girl practice with me. I hoped I wouldn't disappoint her too much. I'm not very girly.

NO PROMISES

Later in the afternoon, I went over to say
thanks to Ethan for being so great with Matt.
He wasn't due to take over from Dr Barnes
until the following week, so he was at home
doing some more unpacking. He just
laughed and said that he hadn't imagined his
first case in Dolphin Shores to be such a

dramatic one. He invited me in and I met Kate. Andrew was right about her being a babe. She was really pretty, and friendly too. In a way, she sort of reminded me of Dad's girlfriend Mel.

She made me a raspberry spider and offered me some chocolate biscuits — which of course I gratefully accepted. I wouldn't have wanted to be rude. We sat and talked about school and Dolphin Shores for a while.

'So I hear it's pretty quiet around here then?' Kate asked.

'Yeah, sure is. Nothing much ever happens. But the people are friendly. I bet half the town already knows your names, and they won't have even seen you yet.'

'Funny you should say that. When I went into the butcher shop, Mr Madden, is it, he called me Kate and said that if I wanted anything delivered, all I had to do was call because he just lives up the street from us.'

'Oh, well I can tell you how he knows

that. You see his wife Irene, well she's good friends with Mrs Burns, and her husband Jim Burns is the postman. He knows where everyone lives. I'd guess he has to read the names on the mail.'

'Oh, OK. So I shouldn't be worried that there's some deranged stalker out there following me around telling all the shopkeepers my name and address?' she laughed.

'No, sorry to disappoint you, but I've never met any serial killers in Dolphin Shores. Not that I know of.'

Ethan was sipping his tea and smiling a strange secret smile, when out of the blue he asked where my dad was. My ears pricked up. Could he be interested in Mum?

I told him the story about Mum and Dad getting divorced and how Dad had moved to Shelley Beach. I said that we saw him every second weekend and that he had a really great girlfriend called Mel — who looked a bit like Kate.

'So does your mum have a boyfriend?' he asked.

'No, well she's not seeing anyone at the moment.' I didn't want to make her sound like some desperate loser. 'It's not like she hasn't had plenty of guys asking her out, but she doesn't want to go out with just anyone.' I stretched the truth a little bit. 'You know she's really the greatest mum ever, and she only deserves the best.'

'Oh, and what sort of guy would you like to see her with — I mean if you had any say in it?' he asked.

I considered my answer very carefully. I wanted to keep him interested of course, but he had to know that anyone who took my mum out had to be very special.

'Well, first of all he has to be good look-ing, because my mum is gorgeous. Then it's important he has a career, and he's handy with the housework. My mum's a really modern woman and she doesn't need anyone who thinks she'll wait on him hand and foot.'

'Mmmm, I see. Is that all?'

'Well, a trendy house and a groovy sports car might help …' Maybe I was pushing my luck.

'I see.'

I think I might have been raving on a bit too much. I caught sight of Kate and she raised her eyebrows at Ethan.

'So do you think I have any of those things going for me, Penny?'

'You? Do you think you have any of those characteristics?' I knew he was teasing me now so I was going to tease him right back.

'I guess you have some. I mean, you seem to have a good job, and this house is great. The car's not bad either. Mmmm, three out of four.'

'Only three. Yeah, I'll have to get myself off to the gym.' He looked sad, but I could tell he was only faking it.

'So is there any chance I could have

your permission to ask her out. Would you mind if I did?' he said.

I couldn't control myself any longer.

'Mind, who me?!' I exclaimed. 'Of course not.'

I could hardly believe he'd said it. Kate laughed. Then she said he'd been talking about Mum all morning.

'But you're not allowed to tell.' He looked at me with an evil stare. Then I laughed. With the ability to give looks like that, he'd fit right into my family.

''Course not. I wouldn't want to spoil the surprise,' I answered.

'And Penny — no promises. I don't even know if your mum likes me,' he said.

'She'll like you. You saved my der-brain brother's life. What's not to like?' I grinned. 'And maybe if you sign up for the gym, you'll make four out of four.'

Ethan threw a cushion at me. He and Kate were fantastic.

I couldn't believe that Matt's grumbling appendix would give us the solution to Code Name Mr Right. And now Dr Ethan James was going to ask my mum out.

I raced back over to Andrew's place. He and Kimi were walking down the driveway with Roll Up tagging along behind — he'd obviously escaped from the backyard yet again! We were supposed to be working on Code Name Mr Right that afternoon. It turned out we could take Rolly and Bimbo for a walk to the beach instead.

'Hey, you guys, you're never going to believe what just happened,' I said, and ran over to give Rolly a great big hug.